The PEACEFUL PLANE

Written & Illustrated by Annie Alwine

BEHAVIOR BOOKS

SPECIAL THANKS
Thank you to Jim Alwine, Madison Alwine, Miles Alwine Dhalia Balmir, Valerie Dorian, M.A., CCC-SLP, Gary E. Eddey, M.D., MPH, ScM, Shaina Gross, M.P.H, Joel E. Hershey, M.D., F.A.A.P, Emily E. Levy, Gabby Murrieta, Natalie Rodriguez, M.D., Jaclyn Wailan, Michael Walsh.

First Edition

Visit ChildrensBehaviorBooks.com

Library of Congress Control Number: 2021915064
ISBN 978-0-9855386-1-3

For Jim, Madison & Miles.

My inspiration and my adventure buddies. I love you.

Way up high in the sky
we will **fly, fly, fly.**

We'll look so small
to everyone's **eye.**

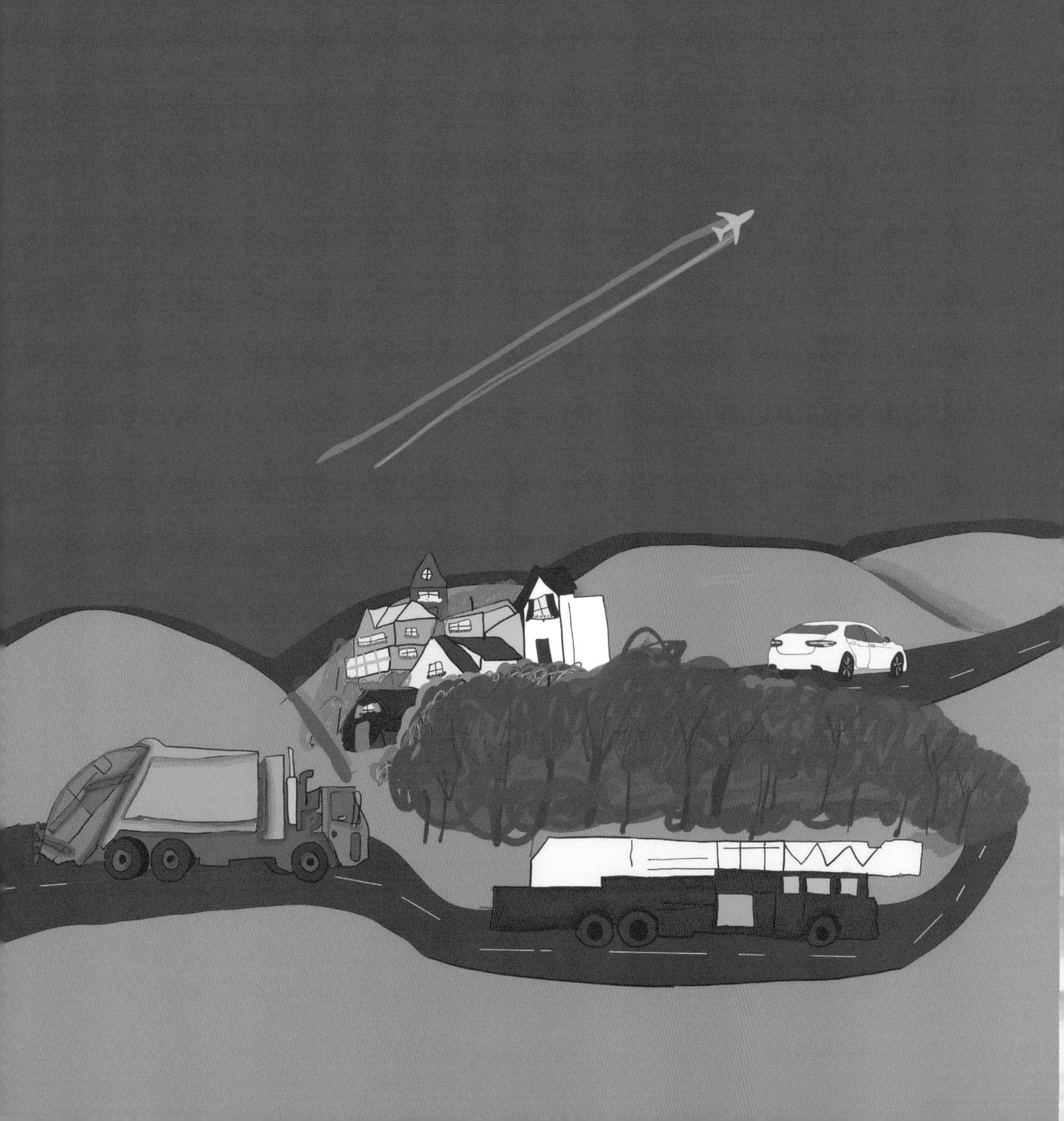

Bye bye, ciao, au revoir, **adiós!**

While at the airport you need to stay very **close.**

Look at me over here,
I'm so **independent.**

We say please and thank you to the
flight **attendant.**

We are soaring at such great **heights.**

Look out the window and see the **sights.**

We stay buckled up safe and **sound.**

As the plane gently hums in the **background.**

During the flight, we stay in our **seats.**

And are very careful not to kick our **feet.**

Turbulence makes us go side to **side.**

Don't be scared, enjoy the **ride.**

It’s best to be courteous and **quiet.**

Or we might upset the passengers and **pilot.**

Our flight adventure is no time
for **groans.**

Watch a movie instead with your
headphones!

If you're feeling antsy and want to **shout--**

Take a deep breath in and

slooooooooowly

let it **out**.

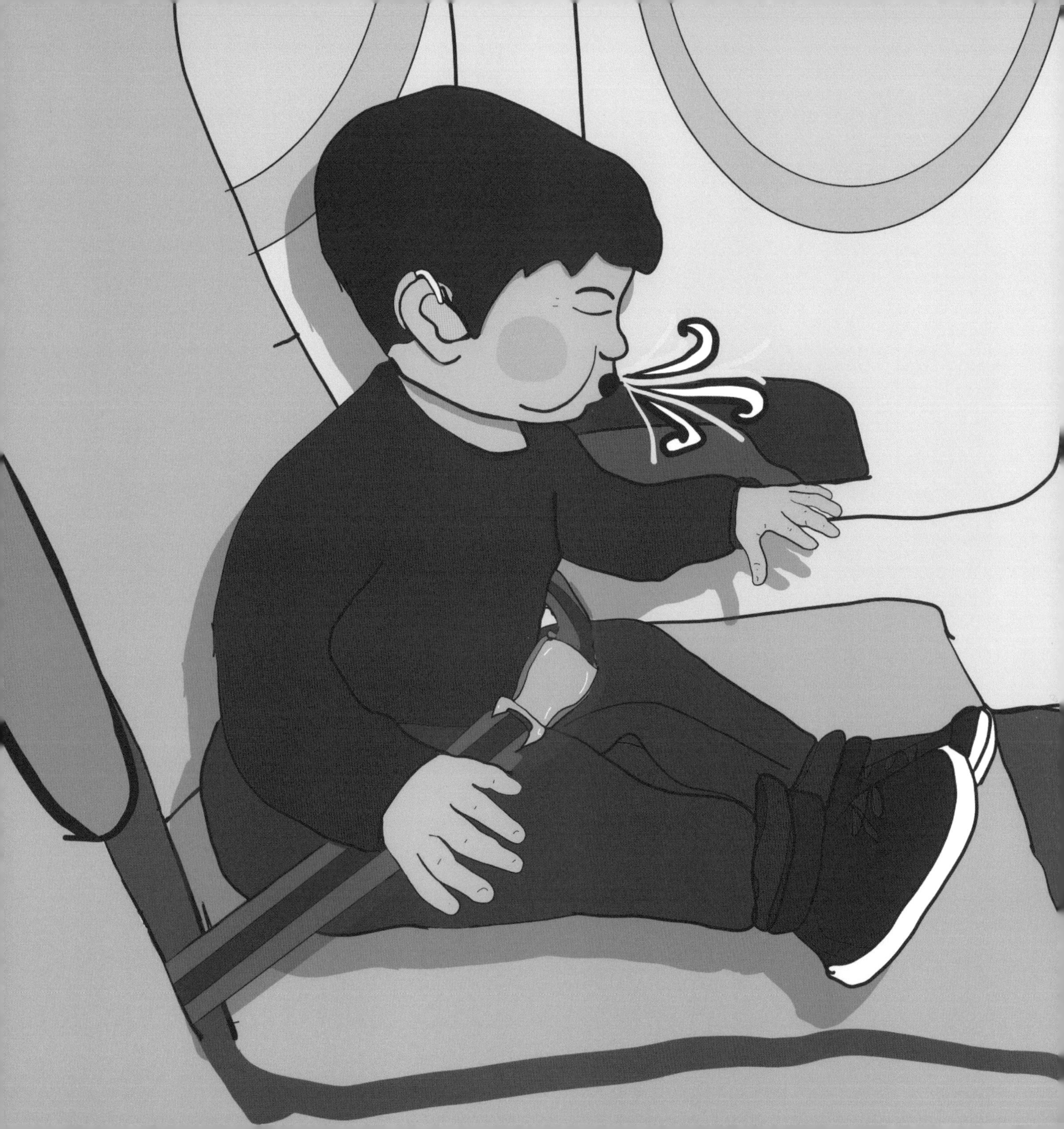

We are landing now! Seats are not **reclined.**

Clean up and don't leave anything **behind.**

Yay! We reached our final **destination!**

Let's have fun and enjoy our special **vacation!**

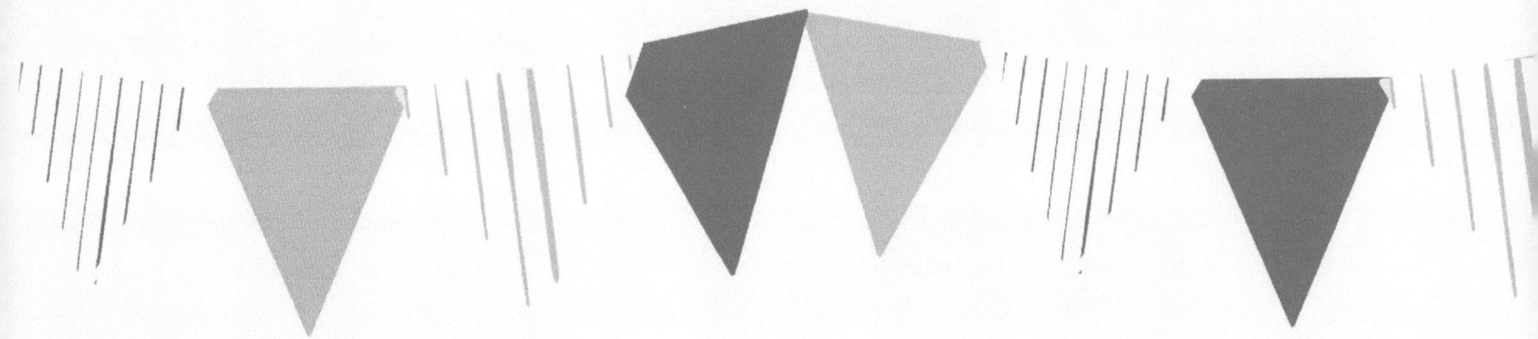

Dear parents and caregivers,

We've all been there when our kids have the case of the wiggles or act out. Usually during the most public and inopportune times. One method for relieving these situations is reviewing your expectations with children beforehand. Children learn through repetition and practice. Here are some questions to get you started. Feel free to add any additional behaviors you'd like to go over with your child.

- Can you name one thing you learned from the story?
- Can I hear your whisper voice?
- Can you show me how we sit on the plane?
- Do you stay near mommy in the airport or do you run away?
- What does the pilot not like?

*Note: all the preparation won't be a match for overtired children. So check out **ChildrensBehaviorBooks.com** or follow us on Instagram **@behaviorbooks** for more resources and tips on flying with little ones.

If you found this book helpful. Please consider spreading the word to help more parents and leave a review on Amazon. Thank you!

Printed in Great Britain
by Amazon